W9-BLD-009
Disney
fairies
PAPERCUTZ

Disney fairies

#2 "Tinker Bell and the Wings of Rani"

Contents

NEW YORK

"Colors of Friendship"
Script: Teresa Radice
Revised Dialogue: Stefan Petrucha
Layout: Daniela Vetro
Pencils: Andrea Greppi
Inks: Roberta Zanotta
Color: Litomilano
Lettering: Janice Chiang
Page 5 Art:
Pencils: Andrea Greppi, Emilio Urbano
Inks: Marina Baggio
Color: Andrea Cagol

"The Lost Fairy"
Script:Teresa Ridice
Revised Dialogue: Stefan Petrucha
Layout: Daniela Vetro
Pencils: Andrea Greppi
Inks: Roberta Zanotta
Color: Litomilano
Lettering: Janice Chiang
Page 18 Art:
Pencils: Andrea Greppi, Emilio Urbano
Inks: Marina Baggio
Color: Andrea Cagol

"The Most Beautiful Dress"
Script: Giulia Conti
Revised Dialogue: Stefan Petrucha
Layout: Emilio Urbano
Clean up: Manuela Razzi
Color: Litomilano
Lettering: Janice Chiang
Page 31 Art:
Drawing: Manuela Razzi, Emilio Urbano
Inks: Roberta Zanotta
Color: Andrea Cagol

"The Wings of Rani"
Script: Augusto Macchetto
Revised Dialogue: Stefan Petrucha
Layout: Daniela Vetro
Inks: Roberta Zanotta
Color: : Litomilano
Lettering: Janice Chiang
Page 44 Art:
Pencils: Emilio Urbano
Inks: Elisabetta Melaranci
Color: Andrea Cagol

"Barefoot"
Script: Augusto Macchetto
Revised Dialogue: Stefan Petrucha
Layout: Daniela Vetro
Inks: Roberta Zanotta
Color: Litomilano
Lettering: Janice Chiang
Page 59 Art:
Clean-up: Andrea Greppi
Inks: Roberta Zanotta
Color: Litomilano

Chris Nelson and Shelly Dutchak – Production
Michael Petranek – Editorial Assistant
Jim Salicrup -- Editor-in-Chief

ISBN: 978-1-59707-226-7 paperback edition
ISBN: 978-1-59707-227-4 hardcover edition

Printed in Singapore. April 2010
by Tien Wah Press PTE LTD
4 Pandan Crescent
Singapore 128475

Distributed by Macmillan.

10 9 8 7 6 5 4 3 2 1

MEET MY FRIEND BESS IN OUR FIRST STORY...

COLORS OF FRIENDSHIP
HOW MANY COLORS CAN YOU SEE IN PIXIE HOLLOW? ONE, TWO, THREE? TO AN ARTIST THERE ARE ALWAYS MORE!
YOU'RE NOT GOING TO BELIEVE WHAT I JUST HEARD!
RANI, RANI, RANI! OH, OH, OH!
HEE-HEE! QUEEN CLARION'S HOLDING AN ART CONTEST, TINK?
OH...YUP! BUT DID YOU ALSO KNOW SHE'S GOING TO PUT THE WINNER ON DISPLAY IN THE LOBBY? DID YOU, HUH, DID YOU?
OR THAT THE THEME IS THE MAGIC OF PIXIE HOLLOW!
I SURE DIDN'T KNOW, TINK!
AND MAYBE BESS DOESN'T EITHER!

BUT WORD HAS ALREADY SPREAD EVERYWHERE, AND THE ART-TALENT FAIRY BESS IS HARD AT WORK.
...MY ENTRY MUST BE, UNIQUE, ORIGINAL AND ONE-OF-A-KIND! OR, WAIT...IS THAT ALL THE SAME THING?
I'VE GOT IT! I'LL PAINT A POETIC VIEW OF HAVENDISH STREAM!
NOTHING'S MORE MAGICAL THAN THE WAY THE STREAM REFLECTS THE SKY! AND I'VE GOT THE PERFECT BLUE RIGHT HERE!
IN A DRIED-OUT BOTTLE? NUTS.
HEAR ABOUT THE CONTEST, BESS?

HI, PRILLA! WHO HASN'T?
THEN HOW'S YOUR ENTRY COMING ALONG? CAN I SEE IT?
THERE'S NOT MUCH TO SEE!
I'M FEELING BLUE 'CAUSE I'M OUT OF BLUE! AND I CAN'T GET MORE ALL ALONE!
ALONE?
YOU'RE NEVER ALONE WITH A FRIEND!
AND SO...
WHAT'S THE PLAN, BESS?
WE'LL GO RIGHT TO HAVENDISH STREAM!
IF I USE JUST THE RIGHT WATER TO MIX WITH MY DRIED PAINT, IT'LL MATCH THE STREAM EXACTLY!

"TO GET IT JUST RIGHT, I'LL NEED A FEW DROPS FROM THE DEEPEST SPOT!"
YOUR BUCKET'S TOO LIGHT!
HMM ...
TONF
BLUB
BUT WITH THAT ROCK, IT'LL SINK LIKE A STONE!
WONDERFUL, PRILLA! THE COLOR WILL BE AS MAGICAL AS THE STREAM IT CAME FROM!
A MAGICAL LOSER, DEARIE!
I JUST SAW DUPRE'S PAINTING–IT'S ALSO A VIEW OF THE STREAM, AND HIS WATER LOOKS LIKE IT'S MOVING! I'D GIVE UP, IF I WERE YOU!

BUT BESS ISN'T VIDIA...
IF YOU THINK ABOUT IT, PRILLA, WE WERE LUCKY TO RUN INTO HER!
REALLY?
NOW I HAVE A CHANCE TO PICK A DIFFERENT SUBJECT FOR MY PAINTING!
A HORSEY? A FLOWER?
NO, SOMETHING EVEN BETTER!
LET'S GO, PRILLA!
BUT YOU'RE SPILLING THE PERFECT BLUE!
DON'T WORRY! WE'RE AFTER AN EVEN MORE PERFECT COLOR THIS TIME! MY NEW PAINTING WILL BE ALMOST ENTIRELY...

"... GOLDEN!"
WOW!
HA! WON'T THE PIRATE'S TREASURE MAKE A GREAT SUBJECT?
AS LONG AS THERE AREN'T PIRATES IN IT!
I JUST HAVE TO GRAB ONE LITTLE COIN... PUFF!
AND SCRAPE OFF SOME GOLD DUST FOR MY PAINT!
SCRATCH SCRATCH
HARR! HERE WE BE, LADS!
TOSS OUR LATEST BOOTY ON THE PILE!
SHHH!!
EEP! CAPTAIN HOOK!
TING

HAR! HOOK KNOWS A COIN TING WHEN I HEAR ONE! WHO GOES THERE?
QUICK, BESS! MAKE LIKE A TREE AND LEAF!
OH, I WAS SO SCARED I TOLD AN AWFUL JOKE!
WORSE, I LOST MY GOLD DUST!
MAYBE VIDIA WAS RIGHT! MAYBE I SHOULD JUST GIVE UP!
NO! PICK THOSE WINGS UP AND TURN THAT FROWN UPSIDE DOWN RIGHT THIS MINUTE!
IT'S USELESS! I'M ALL OUT OF UNIQUE, ORIGINAL, ONE-OF-A-KIND DEAS!
AND THE DEADLINE IS TOMORROW MORNING!

BUT THERE'S LOTS MORE COLORS! YOU COULD PAINT DULCIE'S GLOWING OVEN WITH A FIERY BRICK RED!
EH, I'M MORE OF AN OUT-DOORSY SORT.
HOW ABOUT PAINTING THE GREEN FOREST?
BEAUTIFUL, BUT IT WOULD TAKE DAYS JUST TO COUNT THE DIFFERENT SHADES!
BROWN FOR THE HOME TREE?
SIGH. TOO DARK!
WHITE FOR THE ROCKS IN MERMAID LAGOON?
TOO BRIGHT!

THANKS FOR TRYING, PRILLA, BUT I'VE LOST MY ARTISTIC WAY...
WE'RE LOST IN MORE WAYS THAN ONE! I'VE NEVER BEEN TO THIS PART OF THE FOREST!
WOOOOSH
THAT WIND IS MAKING THINGS PRETTY COLD, TOO...
IT'S AS IF SOMETHING'S COVERING THE SUN!
LIKE THAT SNAPPING BRANCH!
BESS, LOOK OUT!

WHAT THE...?!
FRUMP
TONK
THAT WAS CLOSE!
YOU...YOU...SAVED MY LIFE!
THANK YOU, THANK YOU, THANK YOU! IF IT HADN'T BEEN FOR YOU...
SO I GUESS YOU'RE NOT ANGRY THAT OUR DRESSES ARE ALL STAINED, HUH?

NOPE! THESE BERRIES MAKE A BEAUTIFUL ORANGE!
AND YOU CAN'T SAY IT HASN'T BEEN A COLORFUL DAY!
LIKE I SAID, YOU'RE NEVER ALONE WITH FRIENDS!
THAT'S IT! IT'S PERFECT!
A SINGULAR, UNIQUE, ONE-OF-A-KIND IDEA!
LET'S FLY, PRILLA! I'VE GOT ART TO CREATE!
BUT THE DEADLINE!
DON'T WORRY! I STILL HAVE ALL NIGHT!

THE NEXT MORNING AT THE HOME TREE...
ALL YOUR WONDERFUL WORKS DESERVE A PLACE OF HONOR, MY AMAZING ART-TALENT FAIRIES!
BUT THERE IS ONE IN PARTICULAR I SHALL HANG HERE WITH PRIDE!
FOR OF ALL THE MAGIC IN OUR HOME, IT REFLECTS THE MOST IMPORTANT OF ALL!
FRIENDSHIP!
OOOH!
WHAT SPLENDID COLORS, BESS!
I DON'T DESERVE ALL THE CREDIT...
WHO BETTER TO TEACH YOU ABOUT THE MAGIC OF FRIENDSHIP THAN A GOOD FRIEND! PRILLA SHOWED ME THAT!
AND TO GET IT JUST RIGHT, I HAD TO USE EVERY COLOR IN THE RAINBOW!
THE END

WAIT TILL YOU MEET LILY AND A VERY SPECIAL FLOWER--IN OUR NEXT STORY!

THE LOST FAIRY
SOME CLUMSIES JUST HAVE GREEN-THUMBS, BUT GARDEN-TALENT FAIRIES ARE GREEN ALL OVER!
BRUSH THAT GRASS, LADIES! I WANT TO SEE IT SHINE!
HEAVE-HO!
LILY, THIS CORNER OF THE GARDEN IS TOTALLY AWESOME!
HERBS
HERBS
IF YOU LIKE *THIS*, PRILLA, COME WITH ME FOR A *REAL* TREAT!
WHERE TO?
THIS WAY! THERE'S A SPECIAL FLOWER I'D LIKE YOU TO MEET!

SHORTLY...
IT'S THE ONLY ONE I'VE EVER FOUND... THE *NEVER-EVER FLOWER!*
BZZZZ
EEP! A BEE!
BZZZ
DON'T WORRY! IT'S JUST MY DEAR PAL *BUMBLE!*
IT'S SO HOT TODAY, I ASKED HIM TO FAN THE BUD!
BZZZZ
IS IT DELICATE?
OH, YEAH! AND PICKY LIKE YOU WOULDN'T BELIEVE! I HAVE TO GATHER FRESH DEW FOR IT EVERY MORNING...
...THEN *CARESS* IT EVERY EVENING, AT SUNDOWN!
EVERY EVENING?

WHAT MAKES IT SO SPECIAL?
IT ONLY BLOOMS ONCE EVERY THOUSAND MOONS!
BUT WHEN IT DOES, IT SHINES LIKE THE SUN! AND ITS SCENT IS SOOO WONDERFUL!
OOOH! WHEN WILL WE GET TO SEE IT?
VERY SOON! DURING THE NEXT RAIN, IN FACT!
GREAT!
OH, BUMBLE! AFTER ALL OUR HARD WORK, MAYBE I SHOULD STAY AND SING TO IT UNTIL IT OPENS!
HOW ROMANTIC!
OOH-LA-LA- OO-LA-LA-LA- LA!
ROMANTIC, BUT A LITTLE TONE-DEAF!
LILY! PRILLA! WE'VE GOT AN EMERGENCY!
A BRAND-NEW FAIRY IS LOST!
OH, NO!

"JUST ABOUT AN HOUR AGO, WE HEARD A BABY'S FIRST LAUGH, WHICH MEANS A NEW FAIRY ARRIVED."
TEE! HEE! HEE!
"BUT NO FAIRY SHOWED UP! QUEEN CLARION ASKED ME TO FIND YOU TO HELP SEARCH."
...SINCE PRILLA ONCE FOUND A LOST FAIRY!*
LET'S HOPE I CAN FIND THIS ONE, TOO...ANY TRACES?
*IT ALL HAPPENED IN FAIRIES #1!
SHE LEFT A TRAIL! THAT'S WHERE LILY'S TRACKING ABILITY COMES IN! WE NEED YOU BOTH!
BUMBLE, YOU'RE IN CHARGE! KEEP AN EYE ON THAT BUD, BUB!
BZZZZ
SHORTLY...
THAT'S WHAT THE SCOUTING-TALENT FAIRIES FOUND!
TRAMPLED-OVER GRASS LEADING INTO THE MEADOWS? THEN... SHE WALKED?
THAT'S TYPICAL. SHE HASN'T RECEIVED HER FAIRY DUST YET, SO THE POOR THING CAN'T FLY!

LILY, YOU'RE THE ONLY ONE WHO CAN FOLLOW A TRAIL THROUGH THE MEADOWS!
SHE'S RIGHT! AND WITH YOUR GARDENING TALENT, FINDING MORE CLUES WILL BE A SNAP!
BUT...
BUT...
WHY ARE YOU HESITATING? THERE'S NO TIME TO WASTE!
DON'T TELL ME YOU'RE THINKING ABOUT YOUR FLOWER?
OH, IT'S JUST THAT I'VE DEDICATED SO MUCH TIME TO IT! I HOPE IT DOESN'T BLOOM WHILE I'M AWAY...
BUT I'M SURE IT WON'T! LET'S GO FIND OURSELVES A FAIRY!
THIS WAY?
YES!

UNTIL...
THE TRAIL JUST STOPS!
NOT IF YOU KNOW HOW TO LOOK, TINK!
BEFORE LEAVING THE MEADOW, SHE WALKED THROUGH THESE DAISIES AND PICKED UP THEIR SCENT!
NOW ALL I HAVE TO DO IS FOLLOW MY NOSE! SNIFF!
I DON'T SMELL ANYTHING!

THAT'S BECAUSE YOU'RE NOT A GARDEN-TALENT FAIRY! SHE TOOK A LEFT HERE!
...AND HERE SHE CALLED FOR HELP!
REALLY? HOW DO YOU KNOW *THAT?*
I HEAR HER ECHO INSIDE THE TULIP PETALS! HER EXACT WORDS WERE...
HEY! IS THERE ANYBODY ELSE ON THIS ISLAND? *HELP!*

POOR DEAR! IT'S ALL SO NEW TO HER! WE'VE GOT TO FIND HER!
NEWNESS ISN'T HER ONLY PROBLEM! LOOK!
SWALLOWS! AND THEY LOOK HUNGRY! HOPE OUR NEW FAIRY IS HIDING!
WHY ARE THEY SO RESTLESS?
THERE'S GOING TO BE A CHANGE IN THE WEATHER. CHECK OUT THE CLOUDS!
IT LOOKS LIKE RAIN!
OH, NO! MY FLOWER...
IT COULD JUST GET CLOUDY!

"SOMETIMES T'S OVERCAST FOR HOURS!"
"THEN AGAIN SOMETIMES IT JUST..."
DRIP
"...RAINS."
DRIP
DRIP
DRIP
DARN! IF OUR WINGS GET WET, WE'LL HAVE TO WALK, TOO! HEAD FOR COVER!
LILY, ARE YOU... CRYING?
IT COULD STILL BE IN BLOOM BY THE TIME WE GET BACK!
SURE...EVEN THOUGH IT ONLY BLOOMS FOR TWENTY MINUTES!
ME? OH, NO...IT'S JUST... THE RAIN...
BZZZZ

THE RAIN, IS SOON OVER...
A LOST FAIRY IS MORE IMPORTANT THAN ANY FLOWER! AND I SMELL DAISIES AGAIN! SHE'S NEARBY!
SO ARE THE SWALLOWS!
I SEE HER! SHE'S ALL THE WAY DOWN THERE!
OKAY, WE'LL SPLIT UP! PRILLA, YOU AND I WILL DISTRACT THE SWALLOWS!
AND I'LL GO GET OUR NEW FAIRY!
SQUAWK!
THIS WAY, CUTEY!
DON'T FORGET ME!

SQUAWK!
GIVING UP SO SOON? COME ON, CHASE ME!
POINT YOUR BIG BEAK THIS WAY! I'LL TAKE YOU FOR A SPIN!
HEY! HELLO THERE!
UH... WHO'RE YOU?
I'M LILY, A FAIRY, JUST LIKE YOU! WE'RE HERE TO RESCUE YOU!
THANK GOODNESS! THE BIRDS WERE MORE FRIGHTENING THAN BEING ALONE!
AND SO...
WE LOST THOSE SWALLOWS ALL THE WAY AT THE COVE!
HI! I'M PRILLA!

FAIRY FOUND AND MISSION ACCOMPLISHED!
YOU'RE ALL SO WONDERFUL, THANK YOU!
OH, YOU'D HAVE DONE THE SAME FOR ANY OF US!
I'M SO SORRY ABOUT YOUR FLOWER, LILY!
DON'T BE! I COULDN'T BE HAPPIER!
LOOK WHERE WE JUST HAPPEN TO BE!
RIGHT UNDER A NEVER-EVER FLOWER BUSH!
IT IS THE NICEST THING I'VE EVER SMELLED!
TOLD YA!
WOW! AND OUR NEW FAIRY FOUND A WHOLE FIELD FULL!
THE END

HERE'S A TALE ABOUT BECK--AND TRUE BEAUTY!

SOME DAYS YOU CAN TAKE A BREAK, BUT OTHERS, LIKE THIS ONE, ARE *CRAZY* BUSY, ESPECIALLY IF YOU'RE A SEWING-TALENT FAIRY!
THE MOST BEAUTIFUL DRESS
THEY'RE HARD AT WORK ON NEW CLOTHES FOR THE FESTIVAL OF DAZZLING COLORS WHERE THE PRETTIEST DRESS WINS A PRIZE!
AND EVEN THE *SWEETEST* FAIRY GETS A LITTLE HOT-HEADED WHEN IT COMES TO FINDING JUST THE RIGHT DRESS!
WHAT'S *WRONG* WITH WEARING *THESE* CLOTHES?
SHEESH! THEY'RE FINE FOR PLAYING WITH ANIMALS, *BECK,* NOT FOR A *DANCE!*

I KNOW, TINK, BUT I PROMISED THE BUTTER-FLIES THAT TONIGHT I'D...
NO WAY, NO HOW! TONIGHT YOU'RE COMING WITH US! AND WE'RE GOING TO FIND THE PERFECT DRESS FOR YOU!
HEY, HOW ABOUT THIS WHITE-ROSE NUMBER?
OH, PRILLA, I DON'T THINK I'D FEEL VERY COMFORTABLE IN THAT! IT'S SO... DRESSY!
REALLY? I BET IT WOULD FIT ME LIKE A DREAM!
HOW ABOUT A BRIGHTER COLOR? OR SOMETHING WITH EMBROIDERED DECORATIONS?
I DON'T KNOW! NONE OF IT SEEMS LIKE ME!
FUNNY, I SEE MYSELF IN EVERYTHING!
MAYBE I'LL JUST GO FIND THOSE BUTTERFLIES!
COME ON, BECK! YOU JUST NEED TO SEE ONE DRESS YOU LIKE!
WITH HUNDREDS TO CHOOSE, THESE THINGS TAKE TIME...

BECK ISN'T THE ONLY ONE WITH FASHION ISSUES. AT VIDIA'S HOUSE IN A SOUR PLUM TREE...
NOTHING! NOTHING! NOTHING!
AS USUAL, I HAVE NOTHING TO WEAR!
THIS FESTIVAL WAS THE LAST THING I NEEDED! BUT I'LL BE DARNED--
--IF I LET ANY OTHER FAIRY ON THIS ISLAND SHOW ME UP!
WHICH MEANS IT'S TIME TO GO SHOPPING!
SLAM
AT LEAST SHOPPING USUALLY CHEERS ME UP! GRRRR!

MEANWHILE, BACK AT THE MARKET...
I'M NOT USED TO **WALKING** SO MUCH, BUT THE CROWDS MAKE IT IMPOSSIBLE TO FLY!
TA-DA!
I'VE HAD IT! THERE ISN'T A SINGLE DRESS HERE THAT I...
WAIT...
...I THINK I'M IN **LOVE!!**

FINALLY FOUND ONE? MY FEET THANK YOU!
I LIKE IT! I *REALLY* LIKE IT!
NOW WE CAN GO HOME AND GET READY!
ALL WE HAVE TO DO IS TAKE IT OFF THE RACK AND...!
VIDIA!
THAT'S THE NAME, TINKER BELL, DEAR! DON'T TELL ME I'VE GOT SOMETHING *YOU* OR YOUR FRIENDS WANT? HOW *NICE* FOR ME!

WE SAW THAT DRESS FIRST!
AND I DON'T SEE ANYONE'S NAME ON THIS DRESS!
NOW, NOW! DON'T GO ALL RED, IT'S SUCH A BAD COLOR FOR YOU!
JUST MY HANDS! HAVE FUN TONIGHT! I KNOW I WILL!
YOU GET BACK HERE, YOU...
WE'VE GOT LOTS OF OTHER NICE ONES. WOULD YOU LIKE TO SEE?
NO, THANKS. I'VE HAD MY HEART BROKEN ONCE ALREADY!
THAT...THAT... JUST WAIT TILL I GET MY HANDS ON HER...
DON'T WORRY, TINK, I'LL JUST STICK WITH MY ORIGINAL PLAN!

OH, YES, NOW THIS IS JUST WHAT I NEEDED!
KNOCK KNOCK
WHAT?
TINKER BELL! MY, WHAT...A DELIGHTFUL SURPRISE!
BECK HAD HER HEART SET ON THAT DRESS! IF YOU WERE A FAIRY WORTH HER WINGS WITH AN OUNCE OF GENEROSITY, YOU'D GIVE IT TO HER!
HM...WHAT'S THAT REALLY SHORT WORD I'M THINKING OF? OH, THAT'S IT...NO!
I MIGHT HAVE EXPECTED THIS FROM SOMEONE WHO'D STEAL FAIRY DUST!

JUST TO SHOW YOU THAT WHEN YOU *REALLY* WANT SOMETHING, YOU HAVE TO *TAKE* IT, IF YOU REALLY WANT THIS DRESS...
...COME AND GET IT!
HEY!
NO FAIR! YOU KNOW I CAN'T OUT-RACE A *FAST-FLYING* TALENT FAIRY!
YES, AS A MATTER OF FACT, I *DID* KNOW THAT! *TA-TA*, TINK!
RIPPPPP!

LOOK WHAT YOU DID! MY DRESS IS RUINED!
SOMETIMES IF YOU JUST TAKE WHAT YOU WANT...
IT GETS A LITTLE RIPPED!
NOW, DEARIES, I DOUBT YOU'LL EVEN BE GOING TO THE FESTIVAL TONIGHT!
BACK AT THE HOME TREE...
OOOH! IT'S IMPOSSIBLE NOT TO END UP FIGHTING WITH HER!
WHAT HAPPENED? DID VIDIA GIVE YOU THE DRESS?
I'D LIKE TO GIVE IT ONE MORE TRY... MAYBE SHE'LL LISTEN TO ME!
I WOULDN'T BOTHER!!

ALONE AS USUAL, VIDIA LAYS BACK, UPSET ABOUT HER DAY.
WOW, SHE LOOKS SAD.
SHE HAS NO PATIENCE, NO FRIENDS, NO VIRTUES...
NOW SHE DOESN'T EVEN HAVE A DRESS!
SHE'D NEVER ADMIT IT, BUT PART OF HER THINKS TINK WAS RIGHT, SHE DOESN'T DESERVE ONE.
TAP
TAP
TAP
BUT SOME FAIRIES, EVEN WITH THE FESTIVAL COMING, CAN STILL BE GENEROUS!
TAP
TAP
ER...I HAVE A NEEDLE AND THREAD!

THE FESTIVAL ARRIVES, AND *EVERYONE* IS THERE! EVEN...
VIDIA! TINK! STOP SCOWLING, IT'S A PARTY!
I WILL IF SHE WILL.
AND NOW, THE PRIZE FOR THE *PRETTIEST* DRESS GOES TO...
...BECK!
OOOH!
BECK, HOW? YOU LOOK FABULOUS!
I GUESS SHE DOES.

I JUST WENT BACK TO PLAN A, THE BUTTERFLIES! THANKS, GIRLS!
LOOK AT THOSE COLORS!
A GOWN MADE OF BUTTERFLIES!
GREAT!
CLAP
CLAP
FOR THE MOMENT, PEACE RETURNS, EVEN TO TINK AND VIDIA.
AND THE DANCING HAS JUST BEGUN!
THE END

HERE'S A REALLY SPECIAL STORY ABOUT RANI!

THE WINGS OF RANI
THERE'S NOTHING LIKE AN IDLE DAY TO LET THE MIND AND HEART WANDER.
TO PLAY...
TO DREAM...
...AND WATCH THE RIPPLES GROW!
PLUNK
HA! I BET IF I WAIT LONG ENOUGH, THOSE RIPPLES WILL GET AS BIG AS THE OCEAN!!
PLUNK
PLUNK
AN IDLE DAY IS ALSO PERFECT FOR A PRACTICAL JOKE!

CROAK!
YEOW! NO FAIR! I DIDN'T SEE YOU COMING, YOU CRAZY GREENIE! AND NOW I'M GONNA...
...FALL.
SPLASH
BUFO! I BET YOU WERE A CLOWN IN ANOTHER LIFE!
CROAK!
AND YOU SHOULD KNOW BETTER! MY WINGS ARE TOTALLY DRENCHED!
WET WINGS ARE HEAVY AND CAN DRAG A FAIRY DOWN! THAT'S WHY FAIRIES CAN'T SWIM!
I'M SINKING! HELP!

WELL, ALL EXCEPT A CERTAIN, WINGLESS WATER-TALENT FAIRY NAMED RANI.
SAY, I KNOW WAVES, AND THOSE DON'T LOOK RIGHT! SOMETHING'S UP!
IT'S AMAZING THE THINGS YOU CAN HEAR UNDERWATER, IF YOU LISTEN!
HELP!
HELP!
WITH SOMEONE IN TROUBLE, RANI SPEEDS ALONG...
...ONLY TO FIND A DEAR FRIEND!
OH, NO! IT'S BECK!

IT'S ALL RIGHT, I'VE GOT YOU!
GLURP! I THOUGHT I WAS GONNA DROWN!
YOU'RE NOT THE SORT TO TAKE CHANCES! HOW'D YOU FALL IN?
BUFO DECIDED TO SURPRISE ME! IF I EVER GET MY HANDS ON THAT WACKY AMPHIBIAN...
OH, YOU!
SLURP
HA, HA!
WHO COULD STAY MAD AT A SMILEY FACE LIKE THAT?
PAT
BUT, YOU, RANI, YOU SAVED ME! ISN'T IT GREAT THAT YOU LOST YOUR WINGS!
ULP! I SHOULDN'T HAVE SAID THAT!

SORRY, I MEANT THAT... UH...
DON'T WORRY! YOU'RE RIGHT! IT IS GREAT!
IF I STILL HAD MY WINGS, I COULDN'T HAVE RESCUED YOU!
BUT STILL... UH...
YOU KNOW I'VE ALWAYS WANTED TO ASK YOU ABOUT... THAT DAY...
WHY HAVEN'T YOU?
I DIDN'T WANT TO BRING UP A PAINFUL MEMORY! I MEAN I CAN'T IMAGINE NOT HAVING MY WINGS!
BUT I ALWAYS WANTED TO SWIM! AND IT WAS SUCH A MEMORABLE DAY, LIKE A SECOND BIRTHDAY!
BUT IT WAS ALSO FRIGHTENING! A DAY WHEN ALL NEVER LAND WAS IN DANGER!
I REMEMBER THAT!

"A HURRICANE HAD DESTROYED THE SOURCE OF OUR MAGIC, MOTHER DOVE'S EGG!"
"TO CREATE A NEW ONE WE NEEDED THE HELP OF THE TRAPPED DRAGON, KYTO."
"HE REQUIRED THREE GIFTS, SO QUEEN CLARION SENT PRILLA, VIDIA AND ME TO GATHER THEM."
"ONE WAS A MERMAID'S COMB! BUT SINCE WE COULDN'T SWIM, THERE WAS NO WAY TO REACH THEM!"
THERE'S ONLY ONE CHOICE! CUT OFF MY WINGS, VIDIA!
NO!

RANI... I...CAN'T!
"VIDIA COULD BE CRUEL, BUT FLYING MEANT THE WORLD TO HER!"
SO, YOU'LL HAVE TO DO IT, PRILLA!
ME! I CAN'T CUT HAIR!
NEVER LAND IS AT STAKE! YOU MUST!!
BUT...
SNIFF
HURRY!
THAT HAD TO HURT!
SURPRISINGLY, NO! NOT AT ALL! IT WAS LIKE... A HAIRCUT!
"AND WHEN SHE WAS DONE, SOMETHING WONDERFUL HAPPENED!"
WOW!
I DON'T BELIEVE IT!

THE WINGS ARE CRYSTALLIZING! THEY'VE BECOME LIKE JEWELS!
MAYBE SOMEDAY I CAN PUT THEM BACK ON, BUT FOR NOW...
RANI? WAIT!
SPLASH
"IT WAS A LOT LIKE FLYING, ONLY A LITTLE SLOWER!"
"AND I'D SPENT MY LIFE DREAMING ABOUT BEING AMONG THE MERMAIDS!"
WELCOME, BRAVE FAIRY!

"THERE WAS ONE OTHER DIFFERENCE FROM FLYING. NO AIR."
"BUT SOOP THE MERMAID BROUGHT ME TO THE WIND ROOM WHERE I COULD BREATHE AND WE COULD TALK."
"AND OF COURSE SHE WAS WILLING TO HELP IN ANY WAY SHE COULD!"
THANK YOU SO MUCH! I'D LOVE TO STAY, BUT WE'RE OFF TO SAVE THE ISLAND!
AAAH! SWIMMING IS GREAT, BUT SO'S BREATHING!

RANI! YOU DID IT!
IT WAS EASY AND FUN!
BUT...WEREN'T YOU EVEN SAD ABOUT YOUR WINGS?
I WASN'T!
I WAS REALLY STILL THINKING I MIGHT BE ABLE TO PUT THEM BACK ON! SOON WE FOUND OUR SECOND AND THIRD GIFTS!
THEN WE TOOK THEM ALL TO TORTH MOUNTAIN, WHERE KYTO LIVES IN A CAGE!
DON'T TELL ME YOU WERE HAPPY ABOUT THAT!
"NOT AT ALL! I WAS TERRIFIED! WE ALL WERE!"
RUN, LITTLE FAIRIES, UNLESS YOU'VE COME TO SET ME FREE!
W-W-WE COULDN'T IF WE WANTED TO, KYTO! BUT PLEASE LISTEN!

WE WANT TO MAKE A TRADE!
YOUR HELP IN EXCHANGE FOR THREE GIFTS!
I LOVE GIFTS! GIVE THEM HERE!
NO! FIRST, YOU HELP US! BUT I'LL TELL YOU WHAT THEY ARE!
A FEATHER FROM THE GOLDEN HAWK, A CIGAR-HOLDER, AND A MERMAID'S COMB!
THAT WILL DO, BUT I WANT ONE NOW! THE FEATHER!
"KYTO WAS SLY, BUT WE DECIDED IT WOULD BE FAIR."
"YET, WHEN WE TRIED TO FIND THE FEATHER IT WAS..."
GONE! IT'S NOT HERE ANYWHERE!
IT MUST HAVE BLOWN AWAY! NOW WHAT CAN WE DO?

NO FEATHER? I'LL SHOW YOU WHAT HAPPENS TO LIARS!
WOOOSH
AH!
WAIT! I'VE GOT SOMETHING BETTER!
TWO... TWO FAIRY'S WINGS!
NO, RANI!
OH! THEN YOU'D NEVER BE ABLE TO PUT THEM BACK ON!
YES...

AND THAT WAS A LITTLE SAD FOR A WHILE! BUT THINGS WORKED OUT!
YOU BET!
GIVING MY WINGS TWICE TO SAVE NEVER LAND WAS THE LEAST I COULD DO.
ARE YOU KIDDING? IT'S THE MOST GENEROUS THING I CAN IMAGINE!
IT SEEMED SUCH A SMALL THING AT FIRST.
BUT SOME GOOD DEEDS JUST KEEP ON GROWING!
... LIKE OUR FRIENDSHIP! THAT STARTED SMALL, TOO! WITH JUST A LITTLE HELLO, LIKE THIS!
PLUNK
PLUNK

AND NOW IT'S AS BIG AS THOSE HUGE RIPPLES?
EVEN BIGGER! SEE? IT KEEPS ON GROWING!
NOW THEY'RE ENORMOUS! THAT BIG?
DON'T BE IN SUCH A RUSH... HAVE A SEAT! SIT AND WATCH!
"MAYBE SOMEDAY, RANI, THEY'LL BE AS BIG AS YOUR HEART!"
THE END

PRILLA, YOU WON'T BELIEVE WHAT THE LATEST FASHION TREND IS IN PIXIE HOLLOW!
IT'S NOT HATS WITH STEMS?
NO, SILLY-- ALL IS REVEALED IN THE NEXT STORY!

BAREFOOT
IT'S A LOVELY DAY IN PIXIE HOLLOW, AND A PLEASED QUEEN CLARION IS LOOKING FORWARD TO THE SETTING SUN!
THE SKY'S A PERFECT BLUE! THE GRASS A GRAND GREEN! I CAN'T WAIT TO GET DRESSED AND VISIT THE GAZEBO!
WITH AN AFTERNOON LIKE THIS, I CAN ONLY IMAGINE WHAT THE SUNSET WILL BE LIKE!
YOUR MAJESTY'S NEW OUTFIT IS ALL READY!
WONDERFUL, CINDA! I'LL BE RIGHT THERE!
RHIA, OLD FRIEND, TOGETHER, WE'VE OUTDONE OURSELVES! THE FEATHER DRESS IS SO SOFT!
...THE HANDBAG MATCHES AND THE PEARL NECKLACE GOES WITH BOTH PERFECTLY! NOT TO MENTION THE SHOES!
UH...SPEAKING OF WHICH, WHERE ARE THE QUEEN'S SHOES?
DIDN'T CINDA PUT THEM WITH THE DRESS?

ME? WHAT DO I HAVE TO DO WITH IT?
LAST I SAW, LISEL BROUGHT THEM TO THE POLISHING-TALENT FAIRIES!
MAYBE YOU FORGOT TO PICK THEM UP?
NO, NOT MY DEPARTMENT! GRACE IS IN CHARGE OF THE QUEEN'S SHOES!
B-BUT I'D SWEAR CINDA SAID SHE'D TAKE CARE OF THEM THIS TIME...
MAYBE IN YOUR DREAMS, GRACE!
NOW, NOW, I THINK WE'RE MISSING THE BIG PICTURE HERE!
THIS IS NO TIME TO QUIBBLE ABOUT WHAT YOU GUYS DID WRONG! IF WE DON'T THINK OF SOMETHING, THE QUEEN WILL BE LATE FOR THE SUNSET!
NO NEED TO WORRY, LISEL! IT'S SIMPLE ENOUGH!
I'LL JUST GO WITHOUT SHOES! I'LL BE AT THE GAZEBO BAREFOOT!

REALLY? ARE YOU SURE-- TOTALLY SURE?
IT'S TRUE!
SEE FOR YOURSELF! IT'S NOT LIKE THE QUEEN IS TOUGH TO FIND! AND NOT A SINGLE ROYAL TOE IS COVERED!
MAYBE SHE THINKS IT'S TOO HOT FOR SHOES?
OR MAYBE THE QUEEN'S MAKING A FASHION STATEMENT!
I'M SURE THE QUEEN HAS A REALLY GOOD REASON, WHATEVER IT IS!
OF COURSE!
QUEEN CLARION ALWAYS KNOWS WHAT SHE'S DOING!
SO MAYBE IF WE WANT TO KNOW WHAT WE'RE DOING, WE SHOULD FOLLOW SUIT...UH...FOOT!

MEANING... LET'S ALL GO BAREFOOT! COME ON, BECK, WHAT DO YOU SAY?
GO SHOELESS? WHY NOT? I'M ALWAYS UP FOR A CHANGE, PRILLA!
MY BOOTS COULD USE SOME AIRING OUT, ANYWAY!
YEAH, I WAS GOING TO MENTION THAT!
HERE GO MINE!
ME, THREE!
OH, WHY NOT?
HA! THE AIR TICKLES!
IT'S NICE TO SEE BETWEEN MY TOES! HI, GUYS! LONG TIME NO SEE!

THE NEXT MORNING, THOUGH, WEARING NO SHOES DOESN'T SEEM SO GREAT TO RANI.
I THINK I CAUGHT A... CAUGHT A...A... AAAA...
..CHOO OOOOO OOOO!
COLD! I GUESS DAT GOWING BAREFOOT ISN'T SO GWEAT AFTER ALL!
NOW, I'M STUCK IN BED BWOWING MY DOSE!
I'LL BE OUT OF LEAF TISSUES IN NO TIME!
AND MY NOSE IS DWIPPING LIKE A FAUCET! AHH-CHOOO!

A LITTLE DAB OF GARDEN-GREEN...
DRIP DROP
...AND A TOUCH OF HONEY-YELLOW!
IT'S GREAT! I LOVE MY WALL MURAL! EVEN IF I DO SAY SO MYSELF! HEE-HEE!
DRIP DROP
...ICK!
SPLASH
DARN! MY BARE FEET AREN'T BARE ANYMORE! THEY'RE COVERED IN PAINT!

AND THERE ARE MORE PROBLEMS AFOOT AT TINKER BELL'S!
TONK
TONK
THUNK
THUNK
THUNK
NOTHING LIKE FIXING A POT TO CLEAR YOUR HEAD!
ONE MORE WHACK AND SHE'LL BE GOOD AS NEW!
WHEW! I'VE BEEN AT THIS ALL MORNING! THIS MUST BE THE BIGGEST I'VE EVER FIXED!
DID I MISS ANYTHING? MAYBE A STEP BACK IN MY COMFY BARE FEET TO GET A DIFFERENT VIEW...
EEEP!

NEXT DAY, THE SHOELESS FAIRIES COMPARE NOTES...
NEARLY HURT MYSELF STEPPING ON A LITTLE PIECE OF METAL! I DIDN'T SEE IT AT ALL!
BUT, I PICKED IT UP AND DO YOU KNOW WHAT IT WAS?
ICE CREAM? NO...THAT'S NOT METAL...
COME ON, TINK, TELL US!
IT WAS PART OF AN OLD LADLE I'D BEEN LOOKING FOR FOR AGES!
I NEVER THOUGHT I'D FIND IT! NOW THE LADLE IS GOOD AS NEW!
REALLY? THAT'S AMAZING!
GOING BAREFOOT MAY BE UNCOMFORTABLE IN SOME WAYS BUT AT THE SAME TIME, AT LEAST IT HELPED TINK!
WHO'D HAVE THOUGHT IT?
ACTUALLY, THE SAME THING HAPPENED TO ME!

"I STEPPED IN SOME PAINT AND MADE A HUGE MESS, BUT WHEN I SAW THE PATTERNS MY FOOTPRINTS MADE IT DAWNED ON ME..."
Y'KNOW, THAT DOESN'T LOOK HALF BAD!
IN FACT, WITH A LITTLE HELP, IT COULD BE A WORK OF ART!
NOW MY FLOOR IS AS BEAUTIFUL AS MY WALL, IF I DO SAY SO MYSELF!
HA! NOW THAT I THINK OF IT, THINGS WORKED OUT FOR ME, TOO!
"I DID CATCH COLD, BUT STAYING HOME GAVE ME A CHANCE TO SPEND SOME REAL QUALITY TIME WITH MY GOLDFISH..."
SPLASH
YOU SEE *SNIFF* I... I'VE REALLY BEEN NEGLECTING HIM LATELY *SNIFF* SO IT WAS IMPORTANT FOR BOTH OF US!

CHEER UP, RANI! WE SHOULD CELEBRATE!
UH... WHY?
BECAUSE GOING BAREFOOT LED US TO SOME VERY IMPORTANT DISCOVERIES! FROM NOW ON I'LL TRY TO BE NEATER!
RIGHT! I'LL TRY TO THINK POSITIVE IN THE FACE OF A PROBLEM!
OH! OH, ME TOO! I'LL AIM TO BE MORE THOUGHTFUL OF THOSE AROUND ME, LIKE MY POOR GOLDFISH
SNIFF
A TOAST TO SEEING THE BRIGHT SIDE!
EVEN WHEN YOUR FEET LOOK DARK FROM WALKING IN THE DIRT!
BUT GUYS, DON'T YOU STILL WONDER...
...WHY THE QUEEN WAS BAREFOOT?
YOU'RE RIGHT, BESS! I DOUBT SHE MEANT FOR ME TO STEP ON A PIECE OF METAL!

LISTEN UP, FELLOW FAIRIES! OUR BAREFOOT DAYS ARE OVER!
I JUST SPOTTED QUEEN CLARION FLYING TOWARD HER GAZEBO...
...WEARING A MAGNIFICENT PAIR OF SHOES!
WHAT DO YOU MEAN, FIRA?
TURNS OUT SHE DIDN'T WEAR THEM YESTERDAY, BECAUSE NO ONE COULD FIND THEM!
SO TODAY, THEY WERE FOUND?
NOT EXACTLY! IT TURNED OUT THEY WERE NEVER LOST! NONE OF THE QUEEN'S HELPERS HAD BOTHERED TO TAKE THEM FROM THE SHOE RACK!
EACH OF THEM FIGURED SOMEONE ELSE HAD DONE IT!
I THOUGHT I WAS BAD ABOUT LEAVING THINGS A MESS!
SOMETIMES THINGS GET LOST EVEN WHERE THEY'RE SUPPOSED TO BE!
IT IS PRETTY FUNNY! HA! HA!

THE SOUND OF FRIENDLY LAUGHTER AND APPLAUSE DRIFTS FROM THE HOME TREE...
HA! HA!
HA!
CLAP!
..UP TO THE EARS OF QUEEN CLARION.
HA! HA!
CLAP!
CLAP!
...MAKING THE SUNSET ALL THE MORE BEAUTIFUL!
EVEN QUEENS CAN STILL LEARN LESSONS.
AND TODAY QUEEN CLARION HAS LEARNED A GREAT LESSON INDEED.
SHE LOVES THE SUNSET, SHE LOVES THE SOUND OF FAIRIES LAUGHING...
...AND SHE REALLY LOVES GOING BAREFOOT!
THE END

NANCY DREW

A NEW GRAPHIC NOVEL EVERY 3 MONTHS!

#15 – "Tiger Counter"
ISBN – 978-1-59707-118-5
#16 – "What Goes Up..."
ISBN – 978-1-59707-134-5
#17 – "Night of the Living Chatchke"
ISBN – 978-1-59707-143-7
#18 – "City Under the Basement"
ISBN – 978-1-59707-154-3
NEW! #19 – "Cliffhanger"
ISBN – 978-1-59707-165-9

Also available – Nancy Drew #1-14
All: Pocket-sized, 96-112 pp., full-color $7.95
Also available in hardcover for $12.95 each

NANCY DREW BOXED SETS
#1-4 ISBN – 978-1-59707-038-6
#5-8 ISBN – 978-1-59707-074-4
#9-12 ISBN – 978-1-59707-126-0
#13-16 ISBN – 978-1-59707-174-1
All: full-color, $29.95 each

#1 "The Wind in the Willows"
ISBN – 978-1-59707-096-6
#2 "Tales from the Brothers Grimm"
ISBN – 978-1-59707-100-0
#3 "Frankenstein"
ISBN – 978-1-59707-131-4
#4 "The Adventures of Tom Sawyer"
ISBN – 978-1-59707-153-6
NEW! #5 "Treasure Island"
ISBN – 978-1-59707-184-0
All: 6 ½ x 9, 144 pp. full-color, $13.95
Also available in hardcover for $17.95 each

Please add $4.00 postage and handling. Add $1.00 for each additional item.
Make check payable to NBM publishing. Send to:
Papercutz, 40 Exchange Place, Suite 1308,
New York, New York 10005, 1-800-886-1223

www.papercutz.com

WATCH OUT FOR PAPERCUTZ

Welcome to the second supercalifragilisticexpialidocious DISNEY FAIRIES graphic novel from Papercutz. I'm Jim Salicrup, the Editor-in-Chief and one-time guest on the All-New Mickey Mouse Club. I'm here to generally let you know what else is happening in the Wonderful World of Papercutz, but because we squeezed in so many fantastic stories into this graphic novel, we're virtually out of room!

But do you think a little thing like that will stop me from telling you about another Papercutz graphic novel series we're sure you'll enjoy? Of course not…

One of the most exciting events happening right now is the big 80th anniversary celebration of the world-famous Girl Detective, NANCY DREW by Carolyn Keene. For the past five years Nancy has been starring in her very own series of all-new Papercutz graphic novels, which, believe it or not, is the first time Nancy has ever been featured in comics. We wanted to do something extra special to commemorate her latest literary milestone, and came up with something really exciting. So, in NANCY DREW Graphic Novel #20 "High School Musical Mystery Part One," Nancy Drew finally meets the beloved stars of another Carolyn Keene mystery series—those sister sleuths known as the Dana Girls. Yes, it's true! Nancy visits the Starhurst School for Girls and meets Louise and Jean Dana—just in time to solve a brand new mystery.

If you're a regular NANCY DREW fan then you already know how much fun these Papercutz graphic novels are, but if you haven't sampled the wondrous writing by Stefan Petrucha and Sarah Kinney, who have both written countless classic MICKEY MOUSE comics, or witnessed the simply stunning Sho Murase artwork with your own eyes—then you simply don't know what you've been missing! Go to www.papercutz.com for more information, news, and previews of all the latest Papercutz comics and graphic novels.

And now for a very important message! Please let us know what you think of DISNEY FAIRIES graphic novels #1 and #2. Send your comments to me at: Jim Salicrup, DISNEY FAIRIES, Papercutz, 40 Exchange Place, Suite 1308, New York, NY 10005 or email me at salicrup@papercutz.com. We really want your feedback. Give us your honest opinion—do you love our DISNEY FAIRIES graphic novels? Or are we somehow doing something wrong? Let us know, and we'll run the most interesting comments in a future DISNEY FAIRIES graphic novel.

Also, be sure to visit www.disneyfairies.com to find out what's new in Pixie Hollow for Tinker Bell, Prilla, Beck, Rani, Vidia, Terence, and all the rest. And finally, on the next few pages we proudly present a special preview of DISNEY FAIRIES Graphic Novel #3 "Tinker Bell and the Day of the Dragon"! It's just a small sample of the all-new magic that awaits you. We know you won't want to miss it!

Thanks,

Jim

Special Preview of DISNEY FAIRIES #3
"Tinker Bell and the Day of the Dragon"

AND SINCE EVEN FAIRIES HAVE TO EAT SOMETIMES, THE TABLE-SETTING TALENT FAIRIES SET A PLACE FOR ALL!
EEP! IT'S NEARLY SNACK TIME! HURRY!
WHOA! SORRY!
WHUMP
OH, THAT'S ALL RIGHT, LILY! SIGH!
SIGH? WHAT'S THAT ABOUT?
I'M JUST SO TIRED! I COULD USE A BIT MORE FAIRY DUST!
I'D FLY TO THE MILL MYSELF, BUT I DON'T THINK I CAN MAKE IT!
SAY NO MORE! I'M ON IT!

IN SOME WAYS, THE MILL IS THE CENTER OF ALL THE WORK AT THE HOLLOW.
FOR IT'S HERE THE PRECIOUS *FAIRY DUST* IS GROUND.
AND THE *DUST* ALLOWS THE FAIRIES TO FLY AND WORK THEIR TALENT'S MAGIC.
THANKS, TERENCE! THIS WILL GET HER UP ON HER FEET!
HEY, NO PROBLEM, LILY! IT'S WHAT I DO!

HMM...BUT UNLESS THERE'S A LOT MORE DUST SOON, I WON'T BE DOING IT FOR VERY LONG!
THE MILL WAS WORKING ALL NIGHT... BUT THERE'S BARELY *HALF* OF WHAT THERE SHOULD BE!
GRIND
CRUNCH CRUNCH
GRIND
GRIND
WELL, *THAT* DOESN'T SOUND GOOD.

FUNNY, THE GEARS AND PULLEYS ALL *LOOK* OKAY! BUT THERE'S THAT NOISE!
GRIND
GRIND
CRUNCH
I'D BETTER SHUT DOWN IN CASE SOMETHING'S ABOUT TO BREAK!
CRUNCH
CRUNCH
GRIND
GRIND
THE SOUND IS *STILL* THERE? HOW? AW... *TINKER BELL! PRILLA!*
CRUNCH
CRUNCH
I THOUGHT YOUR CHEWING WAS THE *MILL* BREAKING!
HEY, IT *IS* SNACK TIME, YOU KNOW!
WE THOUGHT WE'D EAT WITH YOU, BUT... *ACHOO!* IT'S *WAY* TOO DUSTY!
AT LEAST I KNOW IT'S *SAFE* TO START THE MILLSTONE!
IS IT?
CRACK
NO! IT *WASN'T* JUST YOUR CHEWING! THAT GEAR MUST HAVE BEEN *WEAK* AND NOW IT'S *SNAPPED!*
GRRRRR

Don't miss DISNEY FAIRIES #3 "Tinker Bell and the Day of the Dragon"!